First published in 2020 by Akashic Books in the *Columbus Noir* anthology, edited by Andrew Welsh-Huggins

Standalone edition published in 2025 by Yo Productions LLC

Yo Productions LLC
7185 E. Main Street, Unit 1543
Reynoldsburg, OH 43068

Visit our website at www.yoproductions.net

Scripture quotations are from the King James Version (KJV) of the Bible, which is public domain.

This is a work of fiction. Names, characters, places, and incidents are either the product of the author's imagination or are used fictitiously. Any resemblance to actual persons, living or dead, events, or locales is entirely coincidental.

ISBN: 978-1-7368659-2-7 (trade paperback)

ISBN: 978-1-7368659-3-4 (e-book)

Cover Design: David Sanders Jr.

For information regarding special discounts for bulk purchases, please contact

Yo Productions LLC at 614-452-4920 or info_4u@yoproductions.net.

Printed in the United States of America

THE VALLEY

a noir short story

YOLONDA TONETTE SANDERS

Yo Productions LLC

Columbus, OH

Acknowledgments

To my framily (friends and family), I love y'all more than I can express. I especially want to thank my babies—grown and young, related by blood and love, or just love—and my husband. David, thank you for believing in me—even when I sometimes fail to believe in myself.

To Andrew Welsh-Huggins, when you first invited me to write for the *Columbus Noir* anthology, I declined due to concern that my writing style wouldn't fit and an unwillingness to compromise. Thank you for not taking "no" for an answer . . . for stretching me, helping me grow, and giving me space to write authentically.

To my agent, Sara, thank you for encouraging me to participate in the anthology. You never stop believing in me, and I am grateful.

I saved the best for last . . .

To the Lord, thank You for finding a way to speak through me, even in the dark.

THE VALLEY

"One one thousand, two one thousand, three one thousand . . ."

Nine-year-old Kellie counted out the numbers, resting her head on her forearm as she leaned against the tree while her friends and brother found their hiding spots. Though her eyes were supposed to be closed, she squinted, peeking just enough to get a general idea of the direction some had gone in John Bishop Park. Kellie couldn't see everyone without turning her head. She resisted the urge to do so to avoid being accused of cheating like last time. Kellie did manage to see where a few people had gone. Andy, a boy who lived down the street, ran behind the tree on her left. Skyla, their neighbor, was crouching at the base of the slide. Jeffrey, her little brother and youngest child in their playgroup, was running around in circles complaining he couldn't find anywhere to hide like he always did.

At six, Jeffrey was only selected to be "it" as a last resort or when he started crying, threatening to tell his and Kellie's parents that Kellie wasn't playing fair. No one, including Kellie, liked to hide with him because he couldn't keep quiet, and he always whined if he got caught before he wanted to. Truth be told, he was a brat, and the only reason Kellie brought him to the park with her was that their parents made her. Reluctantly putting her resentment aside, Kellie closed her eyes and kept counting. Almost immediately she stopped, interrupted by the blast of heavy metal music.

She peeked again, glimpsing two teenagers in a blue van before resuming the game.

"Eighteen one thousand, nineteen one thousand, twenty one thousand. Ready or not, here I come!"

Kellie opened her eyes and at the same moment, she heard a scream. She looked around but saw no one outside of their hiding place. Had she imagined the sound? Stepping away from the tree, she saw the blue van heading for the exit. Kellie made eye contact with the driver for a quick second. He smiled, and she smiled back. Then, to her shock, he laughed and gave her the finger as he peeled out of the parking lot and disappeared down the street.

Confused by the driver's actions and slightly perturbed at the intrusion, Kellie stared after the van for a long moment. Boys could be so stupid. They were also unnecessarily annoying if she included her little brother in her assessment of males. Kellie was pleasantly surprised to see that Jeffrey had apparently found a hiding spot. She smiled. Perhaps her baby brother wasn't as stupid as he was annoying. With the park finally quiet again, Kellie repeated her charge.

"Ready or not, here I come."

Kellie first ran in Andy's direction. He peeked around the tree and saw her coming. He took off toward the base, which was the tree from which Kellie had been counting. She was never going to catch him. Other kids ran toward the base as well, but Kellie was fast enough to tag Skyla as she came from behind the slide. "You're it!"

"Aw, man!" Skyla moaned. Together, Kellie and Skyla walked back to base where everyone took a moment to catch their breath and talk about their hiding spots. Finally, Skyla asked, "Y'all ready to go again?"

The kids were off in a flash as Skyla began counting.

As Kellie jogged away, she looked around for her brother. "Hey, has anyone seen Jeffrey?" No one paid any attention. They were all too busy running for safety. Kellie searched to no avail. There was no sign of him. She was so perplexed she didn't hear when Skyla had finished counting. "Tag! You're it!" Skyla shouted a few moments later, slapping her on the shoulder.

Laughter erupted as other kids ran to the base, teasing Kellie for having been caught so quickly.

"Guys, I can't find my brother," she explained.

"He's probably still hiding somewhere," one of the boys said. "Last time I saw him, he was by the parking lot. I bet he's behind one of the cars."

Kellie ran in that direction. Other kids followed. He wasn't there.

"Let's check the shelter across the street," suggested Andy. He and a few others crossed Etna Road while Kellie stood paralyzed in the parking lot. Pretty soon kids scattered around the park in search of Jeffrey. Everyone was shouting his name. Their efforts were in vain. A pit forming in her stomach, Kellie ran three blocks home to face the wrath of her parents who had warned her to keep an eye on him.

Upon delivering the news that she "could not find Jeffrey," her dad hopped in the car and sped out while her mom quickly called the Whitehall police. Soon, several of the neighbors — adults and kids alike — scanned the streets looking for her brother. Owners of cars that were left at the park for whatever reason were contacted and questioned. Hours of searching turned into days, and after a week, hope was fading. Officers interviewed each kid who was at the park that day, wanting to know every detail they could recall. Kellie told them about the van with the teenage boys, wondering if they were responsible for her brother's disappearance. She left out the part about the scream, afraid it might bring further resentment from her parents about her irresponsibility. Besides, she wasn't sure if she had really heard anything. She kept the detail to herself, even after her brother's body was found in the wooded area, a mile or so from John Bishop Park. He'd been raped and strangled.

><>

One one thousand, two one thousand, three one thousand—

Kellie abruptly awoke. She looked at the clock. 3:13 a.m. Sighing heavily, she reached the nightstand for the two bottles she kept there. She opened the short plastic one, removed two pills, and popped them into her mouth. She opened the tall bottle and took a long gulp of the brown liquid, washing down the pills in an attempt to escape the nightmare from twenty years ago.

The moonlight glow coming through the open blinds of her bedroom window shed enough light that she could read Psalm 23:4 inscribed on her wall. *Yea, though I walk through the valley of the shadow of death, I will fear no evil.* When Kellie was younger, her dad stenciled this verse for her after she'd had a series of bad dreams. *"Remember, God will always protect you,"* he would say. *"Whenever you wake up from a nightmare, I want this verse to be the first thing you see. Allow His word to comfort you."*

Well, that advice worked when she was a child, before Jeffrey's murder, but now she was sure it was the two bottles— the benzodiazepines and the liquor—that really calmed her. For all her parents' religious talk, they failed to internalize it after Jeffrey died. By the following year, her dad had lost his job and caved to alcoholism. Thankfully, he had a small inheritance from his family that kept the mortgage paid and the utilities on. If there was a bright side to things, Kellie would say that she always had a roof over her head and food on the table, even if she had to prepare it herself.

Kellie's mother had passed long ago, losing her struggle with depression by succumbing to suicide nearly three years to the anniversary date of Jeffrey's death. Kellie would never forget the day she walked into the bathroom to brush her teeth, hoping against hope they'd actually purchased toothpaste. She was so tired of using pure baking soda as a substitute. As Kellie pushed the bathroom door open to enter, she could hear a steady drip. It wasn't water as she'd assumed, but blood. Her mother lay in the bathtub, her arm dangling over the side with blood dripping from her wrist onto the ceramic floor. She'd used a kitchen knife to do the damage. In the tub with her was a picture of her favorite child.

No one needed to verbalize that Jeffrey was the favorite of both parents. It was always implied. As the oldest sibling by three years, Kellie was the one scolded for any and everything that went wrong, even if it was Jeffrey who had done it. *"You should have been keeping a closer eye on him,"* one of her parents would say. Or her mother's favorite line, *"If he did do something to you, I'm sure it was in retaliation to whatever you did to him."* Jeffrey could do no wrong in their parents' eyes. After his death, instead of appreciating the fact that they still had one child left, both parents mourned as if Jeffrey had been their only offspring. The beatings Kellie suffered and the verbal attacks after he died were clear indications that they blamed her. After her mom's death, Kellie was pretty much left to fend for herself as her dad was often too drunk to care about her needs. His were all that mattered.

"Kel, come here," he'd called her into his room one night.

"Yes, sir," she'd timidly answered before entering. She'd witnessed him load up on drinks less than a half hour earlier.

Nothing good ever happened when he drank. She knew that. She braced herself for verbal abuse, which was often followed by a beating.

"Come *here,*" he patted the bed next to him and smiled.

Kellie found herself letting down her guard. His voice was soft, not hard as she'd grown accustomed to since Jeffrey died. She eagerly approached the bed and sat down next to her father who put his arm around her.

"Things are going to be different now that your mom's gone. It's just the two of us now, you know that, right?"

Ignoring the stench of liquor on his breath, she nodded. "Yes, Daddy."

Gently, explaining his physical needs and how she was to fulfill them, he slid his hands underneath her shirt to unhook her training bra and instructed her on how to touch his genitals. Paralyzed by shock, fear, and unimaginable emotional pain, Kellie complied with all her father's wishes that night and countless others as the abuse lasted well into her twenties until he'd gotten too sick to function.

Kellie shook her head, trying to erase memories of her sexual experiences with her father, the only man to ever know her in a Biblical sense. Though Kellie now lived alone in this three-bedroom house, she could not remember the last time she'd set foot in her parents' or her brother's room. She was never allowed in Jeffrey's room after he died, and she'd spent enough time unwillingly in her parents' bed being raped by her father that there was no desire to ever walk across that threshold again.

Her father eventually drank himself into cirrhosis before passing away about four years ago, leaving Kellie as the sole recipient of the house and the money that was left from the malpractice settlement he received from the doctor who had failed to inform him of his diagnosis for an entire year thanks to a communication lapse in the doctor's office. If there was one thing Kellie's father knew how to do, it was live well off other people's money. Kellie, too, now lived off those means. As a high school dropout, there weren't many opportunities for her anyhow. She was both uneducated and a loner since all her childhood friendships had dissolved in the years after Jeffrey's death. No friends, no family, no lifelong goals, she spent most of her days watching the Investigation Discovery channel, *Forensic Files*, or the local news simply to ensure that she didn't completely lose touch with the outside world. Kellie found comfort in alcohol, though she wasn't addicted like her father. She told herself she only drank to take the edge off. She was in control—unlike her father.

Kellie read the inscription on her wall once more. *Yea, though I walk through the valley of the shadow of death, I will fear no evil.* She never painted over it because it was a reminder of a time in her life when she was loved by her father in a genuine, untainted way. Recalling his words about protection, Kellie couldn't help but ask, "God, why didn't You protect me from his sexual advances? Why didn't You protect Jeffrey from dying?"

><>

The next day, Kellie stared at the TV in numb disbelief.

"I'm on site at John Bishop Park in Whitehall on the city's east side where a five-year-old boy has gone missing," reported a newswoman. *"Alyssa Jackson told police that she and her children were the only ones at the park earlier today when she left young Mark playing on the swings*

to take his younger sister to the restroom. The mother is certain that she wasn't gone longer than a few minutes. When she returned, her son was nowhere to be found." A picture of the boy flashed across the screen. *"Investigators are asking that if you have seen this boy or have any indication of his whereabouts, please contact the Whitehall Police Department immediately. We'll keep you up to date about this case as details emerge. Allen and Janel, back to you."*

Kellie's stomach knotted, waiting for the shoe to drop. It didn't take long.

"We've been informed that John Bishop Park is the same location where a six-year-old boy disappeared twenty years ago," Allen said, shaking his head with dutiful sadness. *"Jeffrey Sullivan was playing hide-and-seek in the park with his sister and a group of neighborhood kids when he went missing. Unfortunately, his body was found a short time later. Police aren't sure if the two cases are connected. Still, as Leah stated moments ago, please contact the Whitehall Police Department if you have any information."*

"That is so sad," remarked Janel, mimicking her co-anchor's concern. *"We certainly hope there's a better ending for the Jackson family."* Then her face brightened. *"Next up, we'll explain how a new law passed by Congress will affect local gas prices."*

Kellie muted the TV and sought comfort in her bottles. Could this really have happened again? The same park—a boy about Jeffrey's age? She used her cell phone to search for news articles about Mark Jackson. She stumbled across a clip of the boy's parents, pleading for their son's safe return. Putting the phone down, she remembered something.

Rising with difficulty, Kellie stumbled into the dining room, making her way to the table buried beneath papers, books, and unwashed dishes. It took her several minutes but finally she found the file. The typed white label at the top simply read: *Jeffrey*. She carried it back to the couch, sat down heavily, reached again for her bottles, and then opened the file.

At some point in the fog between the end of her father's abuse and his death, Kellie had hired a private detective to investigate Jeffrey's murder. Tim Barnes, a retired Whitehall police officer, had spent a tremendous amount of time looking into Jeffrey's abduction and murder. Kellie had hoped if she could find answers—find the killers—maybe it would appease her father somehow. Maybe he wouldn't hate her so much. Fat chance. Barnes tried but kept hitting dead ends. There simply weren't enough clues out there that the police hadn't combed through three times over.

Kellie had briefly gone through the file a time or two before, but today when she pulled it out, she took her time reading all the articles and notes. There were never any suspects in the case. Kellie—like the police, and Mr. Barnes—didn't think the killers were residents of Whitehall. The community was too small. Someone would have reported a connection with teenagers and a blue van if one existed in the area. Had it been a van she'd seen at all? What if it had been a truck, or perhaps a green van instead of a blue one? As an adult, her subsequent run-ins with the cops over their lack of investigative progress made Kellie question everything she thought she remembered about Jeffrey's case. The only clue she had for sure was the digital sketch of the driver, whom apparently no one else saw but her. The other kids were too busy hiding, she supposed, and Kellie did not get a good look at the passenger. She came to the last two items in the file—a computer-enhanced image of the driver as he might look now that Mr. Barnes had produced at the end of his fruitless investigation, and a single scrap of paper with the name Paul Ackerman written on it.

><>

It didn't take long. Within a week, Mark Jackson's body was found. He had been raped and strangled like Jeffrey, then dumped behind a local thrift store. Shortly after the news of Mark's murder was aired, Kellie sifted through the file again. Before she knew it, she was picking up her phone and calling Mr. Barnes.

"Tim Barnes here, how can I help you?"

"Well, h-hel-*lo*, Mr. Barnes. This is Kellie Sullivan. How are you doing?"

"Doing as well as an old man can, I guess." A long pause. "What about you?"

"I'm fine with a capital F I suppose."

"You sound like you've been drinking."

"Oh, just a little bit," Kellie pinched her fingers together as though Mr. Barnes were in front of her and could see how little she claimed to have drank.

His sigh was an indication that he didn't believe her. "What can I do for you, Kellie?"

"Oh, Mr. Barnes. You sound irritated. Don't . . . don't be like that. I thought you were my friend. You are my friend, aren't you?"

"Listen, sweetheart. I'm busy right now. I'll give you a call later."

"I wanna tell you something important!" Kellie said, trying not to slur her words. "It's real important. Another boy got murdered. And . . .," she lowered her voice, "he disappeared from the same park as Jeffrey." Kellie waited for Mr. Barnes to respond. "Hello? *Hel-lo.*" A look at her phone screen revealed that Mr. Barnes had ended the call. *Jerk,* Kellie thought right before taking another drink.

The sound of her phone's ring awoke Kellie from her stupor. She'd passed out, drooling on top of notes from Jeffrey's case file. She'd known that something had gone wrong, but she wasn't sure what. As she found her phone and a missed call from Mr. Barnes, she started putting together the pieces. Shame and sorrow filled her as she timidly called Mr. Barnes back.

"Tim Barnes . . .," he answered.

"Mr. Barnes, this is Kellie. I'm so sorry about what happened earlier."

"You really should seek help, Kellie. You —"

"I'm sorry, Mr. Barnes, okay? I don't want to talk about whether you think I have a drinking problem or not. I called you about something else. Have you heard about the recent kidnapping and murder of a young boy? He was taken from John Bishop Park like Jeffrey."

"Yes, I've been keeping up with the news."

"Do you think the cases are connected? This boy was found somewhere different than my brother."

"It's a possibility. I'm sure the police will do a thorough investigation."

Heat flushed her cheeks. Prior to hiring Mr. Barnes, Kellie had several drunken encounters with neighbors and others, ending in her arrest for one reason or another. She'd accused several community members of being her brother's kidnapper and killer over the years and had consequently developed a reputation for crying wolf. She hired Mr. Barnes, knowing that if he brought a suspect to the police's attention, they would find him credible. "Would you mind calling any friends you have on the force and asking about any possible links they've found? Me and the Whitehall PD haven't really been able to establish a healthy working relationship."

"I shared with you everything I know. I have other cases and can't get involved at this point," he said softly.

"Fine, whatever!" she spat, finding it hard to hide her disappointment. "I have one more question. I saw on the back of one of the papers that you'd written down the name Paul Ackerman. Who is that?"

He repeated the name and then paused in thought. "He's a longtime Whitehall resident. I found his name on an old message slip with no other information. I don't know who wrote it or why. I went to see him, but he was suffering from Alzheimer's, and his wife didn't know any reason why his name would have been connected with the case."

"Do they have any children?"

"A son, as I recall, but Mrs. Ackerman said he was in his sixties and has lived in Missouri since graduating from college. The Ackermans themselves were in their eighties. Neither the father nor son would have been close to the age of the teenager you saw." Barnes sighed. "I wish I would have gotten a chance to speak with Paul Ackerman when he was still in his right mind. Now, whatever information he may have had is forever locked up in his head."

"That's unfortunate," Kellie replied.

"I suppose. But who knows if it has any bearing on the case. Listen, I have to run. Please take care of yourself. I'm concerned about you, Kellie. You can't keep drinking like this or . . ." Mr. Barnes stopped short of finishing his sentence, but Kellie knew what he would say. Contrary to what he thought, Kellie was nothing like her father.

"Thanks for taking the time to speak with me, Mr. Barnes."

"No problem, sweetheart."

She hung up and decided she would do some investigating on her own. But first, she needed another drink.

Kellie drove up and down Yearling Road past the police station several times, wondering if she should stop. Nope. The cops would likely dismiss her as they'd done many times previously. Instead, she turned off Yearling and pulled up in front of the address she'd found for Paul Ackerman. The house sat on a corner about a block or so down the street from Etna Road Elementary School. She rehearsed what she'd say. Yesterday, between drinks, she spent countless hours looking for unsolved child murders in Missouri. One came up from thirteen years ago when a nine-year-old boy was found along the interstate in Springfield. He had been raped and strangled. There were no suspects. No witnesses. No leads. While it could have been a coincidence, Kellie wanted to be sure. Since Mr. Barnes wouldn't help her, she'd decided to take matters into her own hands and see if she could get Mrs. Ackerman to give her additional information about her son. Once Kellie got what she needed, she'd contact Mr. Barnes. If she did so now, she'd be lectured about not getting involved and how she needed to get help for her "drinking problem."

After taking several deep breaths, Kellie found herself drinking more courage from the little flask that she kept in her purse. She *didn't* have a problem. The liquor burned her throat on the way down. After the sting settled, she blew out one long sigh, exited the car, and headed up the Ackermans' driveway.

The screen door was open and a young girl — ten or so — was standing in the living room playing some kind of dancing video on her game system. Kellie knocked lightly, not wanting to scare the girl.

"Yeah?" she said, looking up but not moving from her spot.

"Hi. I'm looking for Paul Ackerman."

"Dad!" the girl yelled. "Some lady is here asking about Great-Grandpa." When no one responded, the girl took off around a corner without saying anything. Moments later, she returned with a man Kellie assumed was her father.

"Can I help you?"

Kellie swallowed, looking at the man, recalling the age-enhanced photo in the file she'd received from Mr. Barnes. Besides the pinched nose and dark hair, he didn't look much like the sketch or the photo. She wondered if she was on the verge of accusing an innocent man as she'd done many times in the past, but the steady flow of alcohol that day caused boldness to shoot through her veins. She was already here. Why not let this confrontation run its course?

"Lady," the man said. "Something I can do for you?"

His curt tone deflated her confidence a bit. "Um. . ." *Man, did she need that flask right about now.* "I'm looking for Paul, um, Paul Ackerman."

He gave her a weird look. "And you are?"

"I'm, um, Kellie. My name is Kellie."

"Honey, I'll be back. I need to pick up your grandmother's prescription," a woman announced as she walked around the corner. "Oh, hello," she said upon seeing Kellie, then looked at her husband for an explanation.

"This lady is looking for Grandpa. I don't know why yet. I got as far as learning that her name is Kellie."

His wife looked at him strangely. "O-*kay*." She turned back to Kellie. "Nice to meet you, dear, but I have an errand to run. Now, if you'll excuse me . . ."

Kellie moved aside so the woman could leave. The young girl had resumed playing her dance game as soon as her dad came to the door. The music seemed louder than it had when Kellie first arrived. Maybe the girl was trying to drown them out. The man watched his wife back out of the driveway in the SUV that Kellie noted had a Missouri license plate.

"What part of Missouri do you live in?" Kellie asked.

"Excuse me, I don't mean to be offensive, but you reek of alcohol. Are you okay? Can I help you in some way?"

"Don't try to sweet talk me, mister, and change the subject." Kellie pointed a finger at him. "I asked you a question."

"You ask a lot of questions, but I still don't know why you're here. Let's start there. Please tell me what you want with my deceased grandfather."

She hadn't thought about the possibility that Mr. Ackerman was no longer living or the fact that if he was still alive, he'd be afflicted with Alzheimer's. "Oh, I didn't know," Kellie responded, wanting to kick herself for not thinking things through thoroughly before coming.

"Interesting . . ." He opened the screen door and stepped in front of her. Kellie moved back a few steps to create extra distance. "He's actually been dead about a year. Not that it's your business, but my wife and I are here to help my grandmother pack up and move to Missouri with us."

"Is your father available? Maybe I can speak with him . . . or perhaps, your grandmother."

He smirked. "My, my, you seem to want to talk to everyone in my family, but me. I'm Mason, by the way." He held out his hand, though Kellie refused to shake it. "My grandmother isn't up to speaking at the moment. I hate to be the bearer of bad news, but I'm the only male Ackerman still alive. My dad and brother died many years ago in a car accident. You're pretty much stuck speaking with me, but I have to tell you that I'm about three seconds from calling the police. Your instability is concerning me."

The last thing Kellie needed was another run-in with the Whitehall PD, but her liquid courage fueled her, and she found herself confronting him. "Don't threaten to call the police on me. I should be calling them on you! I know who you are."

"Well, of course you do. I just told you my name."

"I know what you did to my brother twenty years ago. I was there." She took pleasure from seeing his smugness fade. "I also know what you did to Mark Jackson last week and a little boy named Ian Valtrose in Missouri. I'm sure there are others."

Mason narrowed his eyes. "Lady, I don't know what you *think* you know, but if I were you, I'd be careful about making such accusations. Someone is liable to get hurt." He looked back at his daughter who was dancing away. "Besides . . ." he turned to Kellie with renewed arrogance, "if there was proof of a connection with any of these people you mentioned, the police would be here, not you. So, Kellie, if that's really your name, I think it's best if you leave now. You obviously have some other issues, and I have lost interest in this conversation. You have until the count of ten to get off my grandmother's property or *I* will call the police," he threatened as he pulled his cell phone from his pocket.

As Mason began counting, Kellie took a step backward, afraid to turn away from him in case he was indeed a killer. Even if he was, it wasn't likely that the man would harm her in front of his daughter, but she didn't want to take any chances. If he was the killer, he had snatched at least three boys from parks in broad daylight. She was sure he'd had help in Jeffrey's case. Maybe his brother? If what Mason said about his brother and father being dead was true, then his brother could never be questioned.

When Kellie got to the edge of the driveway, Mason was on number seven. She felt she was a safe distance away from him that she could turn around and get to her car. Once inside, she felt foolish. That man wasn't her brother's killer. She owed him a great deal of gratitude for entertaining her for as long as he had and saving her from another embarrassing arrest. Kellie would not tell Mr. Barnes about this incident under any circumstances. She would also send Mason an apology card like she'd done the others. No longer angry, but ashamed, Kellie looked up at Mason one last time, smiling apologetically. He smiled in return and then, gave her the finger, just as her brother's killer had done twenty years earlier!

><>

When Kellie was safely in her own driveway, she pulled out the flask and took several swigs, some of the liquor spilling because she was shaking so much. Back inside the house, she decided that the best thing to do would be to call Mr. Barnes immediately . . . after she poured a drink.

"This is Tim. Please leave your name, number, and a brief message after the beep. I will return your call as soon as possible." This was the third time Kellie had called Mr. Barnes that evening since her confrontation with Mason Ackerman, but now she couldn't leave a message because the voicemail was full.

"Ugh!" she screamed, wanting to throw the phone. Instead, she took another drink and kept trying. Eventually, she fell asleep. A few hours later, she woke up and saw she'd missed a call from Mr. Barnes. She played his message.

"Hey, Kellie, I see you've been trying to reach me. I won't be available for the rest of the evening, so I'll give you a call tomorrow. I hope everything is okay."

"No! Everything is not okay," she yelled in response. Frustrated, Kellie had no choice but to accept the fact that she'd have to speak with him tomorrow. She was going to call him first thing in the morning. It was getting late, and she needed to sleep off this lingering headache brought on by the stress of today's events. As she climbed into bed, she thought about how she hadn't bought into the whole religious thing since she was a child. Psalm 23:4 was probably the only Scripture she really knew, and that's because it was on her wall. Nevertheless, she found herself praying. "God, Mason Ackerman killed my brother and those other two boys. I know it. Please don't let him get away with this."

She thought of something someone said on one of the murder mystery shows she watched. A man had spent thirteen years locked up for a crime he didn't commit. DNA evidence eventually freed him. When asked if he was angry about his wrongful imprisonment, the guy said "No." He believed that prison had been the best thing for him. Although he didn't commit the crime for which he had been accused, the guy noted that he was headed down a destructive path and likely would have ended up incarcerated anyhow. *"In the darkest season of my life, I found light,"* the man stated, referring to his salvation.

At the time, Kellie was astonished by the depth of his faith. At one point, her parents had professed to be Christians, but somehow both lost their way. *Why didn't their faith sustain them?* she wondered. As a child, Kellie, too, at one time, was a believer, but life had choked any potential that her child-like faith had of growing. Like the man in the documentary, she had been imprisoned, albeit metaphorically, for a crime she hadn't committed. Maybe she, too, could find light amid such a dark life story. She wanted to give it a shot. As she settled into bed, she looked at the two bottles on her nightstand. Oddly, despite all the craziness of the day and the certainty that Mason Ackerman was a killer, Kellie had a sense of peace. At least for the moment, she didn't need any help drifting off to sleep.

><>

One one thousand, two one thousand, three one thousand—

Kellie was abruptly awakened. Something was wrong. She couldn't breathe. Pain shot through her body as she gasped for air. Someone was choking her. She tried to move her arms, but her assailant had them pinned underneath his body and he was literally squeezing the life out of her. As her eyes adjusted to the darkness, she saw the outline of her attacker's face. It was Mason Ackerman.

How did he know where to find her? As quickly as the question sprang up, she devised a likely answer. When she confronted him, she said that Jeffrey was her brother, and she had foolishly given him her real name. Whitehall was so small that he could have found her address with the simplest of Internet searches. Maybe he even drove around the community and saw her car in the driveway. It didn't matter. He was here now, strangling her like he'd done to Jeffrey, Mark Jackson, the boy in Missouri, and who knows how many others.

Kellie looked past the killer to the inscription on her wall. Though Mason was taking her life, she was not afraid. She was at peace, only disappointed that she hadn't been able to connect with Mr. Barnes. She prayed that he would not give up until he found her killer. Mason Ackerman needed to be stopped. She hoped that she would be his last victim.

As Kellie sank further and further from consciousness, she saw the malevolent look in Mason's eyes. She had only one final thought as she faded away, *Yea, though I walk through the valley of the shadow of death, I will fear no evil.*

Discussion Questions

for

The Valley

1. Psalm 23 is woven into the story. How does this Scripture shape the tone or themes of the narrative?

2. How reliable are childhood memories, especially those tied to trauma? What factors might influence how we remember pivotal events?

3. What are the advantages and disadvantages of living in a close-knit community during times of crisis?

4. In what ways does trauma influence the way characters view faith, family, and community?

5. Discuss the concept of justice versus revenge in the story. What drives someone to seek answers decades after a tragedy, and where is the line between seeking justice and seeking vengeance?

6. What does the title The Valley suggest to you beyond the direct biblical reference?

7. How does the noir style affect your reading of a story that deals with such heavy themes?

Like *The Valley?* Scan the QR code to explore more books and products on www.yoproductions.net.

Connect with Yolonda online:
X: @ytsanders
Instagram: @ytsanders
YouTube: @YoProMedia
Facebook: facebook.com/yoproductions

About the Publisher

Yo Productions LLC was founded in 2008 by Essence® bestselling author Yolonda Tonette Sanders. The company's mission is to create, review, and publish works that S.H.I.N.E. — **S**timulate Minds, **H**onor God, **I**nspire Others, **N**ourish Hope, and **E**ncourage Growth.

As a **literary services** provider, Yo Productions specializes in proofreading, editing, ghostwriting, and consulting to address each client's unique needs. The company has offered creative writing workshops and hosted its signature Weekend Writeaway retreat to encourage relaxation and creativity among both established and aspiring authors.

As a **theatrical entertainment** provider, Yo Productions presents thought-provoking, dramatic performances that reach audiences from all walks of life. The company's motto, "Performance with Purpose," reflects its commitment to produce works with meaning beyond mere entertainment.

As a **publishing consultant,** Yo Productions guides authors through the complete publishing process, from manuscript to market-ready publication, including e-book design services. The company connects authors with print-on-demand distribution reaching over 40,000 retailers and libraries worldwide. Yo Productions provides expert formatting guidance and personalized support, treating every project like a bestseller.

To learn more or submit your work for consideration, visit www.yoproductions.net.

Please enjoy the following excerpt from *Soul matters* (20th Anniversary Revised Edition) by Yolonda Tonette Sanders.

Chapter One

The Perfect Package

It was ten minutes to three, and Wendy was eager to leave work on time. "Start cleaning up now," she said to her first-grade class. They had crayons, markers, and books all over the place. "Be sure to put everything back where it belongs. After you finish, line up at the door and wait until the bell rings."

Much to Wendy's surprise, her instructions were followed with little resistance. A few students mumbled about not being able to finish what they were doing. Still, even they cooperated without her saying anything else. Maybe they could sense that something was different about her. Toward the end of each day, the children usually had exploratory time and could choose between various activities such as reading, coloring, playing educational games, or anything else that Wendy deemed appropriate. She usually walked around the classroom and interacted with several students during that time. However, she sat at her desk like a watchdog this entire week, responding only when needed.

"Just a few more days . . ." Wendy murmured to herself. Next Wednesday, the school would be closed for Christmas break, and as much as she hated to admit it, she was looking forward to having some time off. Although only seven weeks pregnant, she was beginning to feel the effects of this pregnancy on her body. She used to have the vitality of a three-year-old, but lately, she felt like she would lose in a walking race against Methuselah. She was convinced that the term "morning sickness" was deceptive. If the feelings of nausea, vomiting, heartburn, and headaches were only confined to a few hours of the day, it would make the first trimester of her pregnancy much more bearable. Instead, she was liable to experience *morning* sickness at any given moment of the day.

While the children were cleaning up, Wendy was on the edge of her seat, waiting for the bell to ring. *Thank God it's Friday.* She didn't think she would be able to make it another day. She was going straight home after work. She would not leave the house until it was time to go to church on Sunday morning. After service, Wendy planned to go over to her parents' house to celebrate her father's birthday. Wendy hoped to feel better by next Friday when she and her husband, Kevin, were scheduled to go to Philadelphia and visit his family for the holidays. The Ohio native would rather spend her Christmas vacation recuperating from her ailments in the comfort of her own home, but there was no way she could back out of the trip now. Her mother-in-law was ecstatic about the pregnancy and could not wait until they got to Philly so she could show Wendy some of the things that she had already bought for the baby.

"Keep your hands to yourselves," she said to two boys who were shoving each other.

"He started it!" David stated, pointing at Jeffrey.

"Nuh-uh, he did!" Jeffrey pointed back at him.

"It doesn't matter who started it. Both of you knock it off," Wendy replied sternly. Secretly, she knew that David probably was at fault, but she didn't feel like investigating the issue. David was bigger than the other first graders in both height and weight. Jeffrey was one of those children who looked like he had been born premature, making him an easy target for David. Even though David was sometimes a bully, Wendy liked him, probably because he reminded her of herself.

Wendy had never been a bully, but she had been heavy and tall as a child. She used to feel awkward standing next to other children in her class. It irritated her when adults would ask how old she was and then say, "You look like you should be older than that." It wasn't until the summer before her freshman year of high school that she began to thin out. In her adult years, Wendy managed to remain a size eight, but she had to work hard at it, contrary to her younger sister, Kim, who naturally wore a size six.

When the bell rang, it was music to her ears. "Okay, let's go." Wendy jumped up and escorted her class to the pick-up area. Once there, another staff member stayed with them until their bus or a parent came to pick them up. When they reached their destination, Wendy said goodbye to her students and headed back to her classroom.

"Attention, all teachers and staff: Mrs. Phillips, please come to the office. Wendy Phillips to the front office, please," she heard Donna Burchett, the office secretary, announce over the PA system.

For what? Maybe I should go ahead and leave. No one would be able to say for sure that I was in the building during the announcement. Wendy was only a few doors away from her classroom, so all she had to do was grab her stuff and head home. However, she reluctantly turned around and walked toward the office at a medium pace. Her shoulder-length hair often bounced as she walked. Today, it was pulled back in a ponytail. Wendy hated ponytails and only wore her hair in that style when she worked out. However, since she had been experiencing morning sickness, she devoted less time to her appearance. She even had her glasses on, and Wendy normally wouldn't be caught dead in a pair of glasses.

"Wendy Phillips, please come to the office," Ms. Burchett repeated.

Coming! she wanted to yell. *I hope it is something simple like a signature needed on some paperwork that I filed.* She dreaded the possibility of a parent waiting to speak with her about a child's behavior.

"Hi, you paged me?" Wendy inquired as she burst through the door into the administrative office.

"Yes, dear, you had a telephone call," Ms. Burchett replied, exposing the gap between her stained teeth resulting from years of smoking.

"A telephone call? From whom?" Wendy asked, scrunching her eyebrows to indicate confusion. No one *ever calls me at work.* Her friends and family knew she taught and was unavailable during the day. "It must be from a parent. I'll take the message, but I'm not calling anyone back until Monday."

"No, honey, it wasn't from a parent. Someone called from Dr. Korva's office."

"Oh," she said nervously, trying hard to keep her composure and not panic.

"I wrote down the number." Ms. Burchett handed Wendy a piece of paper and pointed to the phone on her desk. "You can call from here if you'd like." She carefully studied Wendy's response.

"That's okay. I'll wait and call later since I'm getting ready to leave anyhow."

"The lady didn't tell me why she was calling, but it sounded important."

Wendy could tell that Ms. Burchett was fishing for information. Odds are, she had already tried to gather as much as she could from the person who called. Wendy hadn't told anyone at the school about her pregnancy yet, and now was not the time to make that announcement. "Thanks so much,

Ms. Burchett, but I'm sort of in a hurry, so I'll call back from my cell phone on my way home."

"Okay. I just hope everything is fine," she said with narrow, bluish-green eyes peering from the top of her glasses. "Are you sick, honey?"

"No, ma'am," Wendy said honestly. Her mind was so boggled with getting to a phone to return Dr. Korva's call that the feelings of morning sickness had been temporarily suppressed.

"Then why would someone from a doctor's office call you?"

As much as Wendy wanted to tell Ms. Burchett to mind her business, she couldn't. The woman was at least in her late fifties or early sixties, and Wendy couldn't strike up the nerve to tell her off. *If only I were a little more like Kim,* she thought, because her sister would not have wasted any time putting Ms. Burchett in her place. The two sisters had similar characteristics with dark brown hair, brown eyes, and dimples. However, Wendy's complexion was just a little lighter than Kim's, and she was also a few inches taller than her younger sibling. Both ladies favored their mother, but Kim had been blessed with a high metabolism and the ability to speak her mind audaciously. Wendy wasn't as outspoken. Besides, she generally liked Ms. Burchett, although this interrogation tested her patience. "I'm not sure, but I'd better run so I can find out, huh? You have a good weekend, Ms. Burchett," she said, backing toward the door.

"Okay, you too—and I'll talk to you on Monday."

Not if I can avoid it, you won't! Wendy walked out of the office and raced back to her classroom. She was so disturbed by the call that she rushed past several of her co-workers without speaking. *Why did Dr. Korva call me at work?* She didn't know, but she was desperate to find out.

When Wendy returned to her classroom, she grabbed the cell phone out of her purse only to discover a message waiting. That was nothing unusual because her phone stayed on vibrate during the day. A lot of times, Kim called her from the hair salon where she worked and left messages when she was between clients.

"Hi, Wendy, this is Susan, Dr. Korva's nurse. She would like you to come into the office today, if possible, to discuss your test results. She's leaving around four this afternoon. If you can't make it before she leaves, then you need to come sometime early next week. Please call the office and let the receptionist know what works best for you. The number here is 555-3794. We hope to see you soon."

Wendy's heart sank. *Dr. Korva told me that they take blood and vaginal swabs to run tests on all expectant mothers. The only reason they would call was if something came back abnormal.*

She looked at her watch. The time was now three fifteen. It would be a stretch to make it from the southeast side of Columbus to the northern suburb where her gynecologist's office was located. Such a trip would take forty minutes this time of day, at the very least. Still, she tried to call the doctor's office anyway, hoping that, with any luck, they would squeeze her in.

Shaking and short of breath, Wendy wiped her sweaty palms on her clothing and dialed the number. "Hi, this is Wendy Phillips," she said, trying to hold back tears. "I'm returning a call to Dr. Korva. Will she be able to see me today? I can be there in about half an hour?" She altered her traveling time, hoping to increase her chance of being seen.

"Oh," she said solemnly when the receptionist said Dr. Korva was running behind schedule. Wendy couldn't be seen until Monday morning. "Well, can you tell her I'm on the line? Maybe she can just tell me the results over the phone." She crossed her fingers, praying that she would be transferred to the doctor. No such luck. Dr. Korva preferred to talk in person. "Okay, I'll be there at nine on Monday," she said, confirming the time of her appointment before hanging up the phone in despair.

How am I going to make it until then? She dreaded going back to the office and arranging for a substitute through Ms. Burchett. *Forget it. I'll just call in,* she opted. Sure, not submitting a request for a substitute beforehand was inconsiderate and unprofessional, but she didn't care at this point. Her main concern was finding some way to make it through the weekend without losing her mind.

Wendy got her stuff and headed for the car. She tried to talk herself into remaining calm, but it wasn't working. She felt lightheaded. *What if my baby has a mental disability? What if it's deformed or has some kind of genetic defect?* She tormented herself. She was afraid of what the doctor would say. She knew it was bad news. Her fear turned into anger toward Kevin. *I told him that his smoking could cause damage to the child, but he didn't believe me.* If Kevin just smoked cigarettes, she could probably deal with it a little better, but he sometimes smoked marijuana, and Wendy couldn't stand it.

Whenever she complained about his recreational activities, Kevin got upset. He would tell her that he was not doing anything that she wasn't aware of before they got married. True, Wendy knew about his smoking when they were dating, but it was different then. She was attracted to his street-but-sweet personality. She had never dated anyone so successful, yet a little rough around the edges. Plus, he was very pleasing to the naked eye. He reminded her of a Denzel Washington wrapped up in a Barry White voice. He was the perfect package: sexy, successful, and single.

Kevin's accomplishments intrigued her most of all. He worked hard for everything he owned and built his real estate business from the ground up. He was very successful and made well over six figures a year. He didn't have parents who could afford to pay for his education. He paid for it himself. He didn't grow up in the suburbs of some major city but lived in various ghettos of Philadelphia. His father left home when Kevin was only three, and his mother raised him, his older brother, and his sister with money she received from the federal government. He didn't let his life's circumstances prevent him from making something of himself, and Wendy respected that.

Foolishly, she convinced herself that Kevin would change the things that she didn't like about him once they married, but he hadn't. Now, nearly six months into the marriage, the

Excerpt from *Soul Matters* by Yolonda Tonette Sanders

honeymoon was over, and reality had settled in. *If something is wrong with the baby, I know it'll be all his fault,* Wendy told hersel

Please enjoy the following excerpt from *Connecting with Christ: 52 Weekly Devotionals to Nurture Spiritual Growth* edited by Yolonda Tonette Sanders.

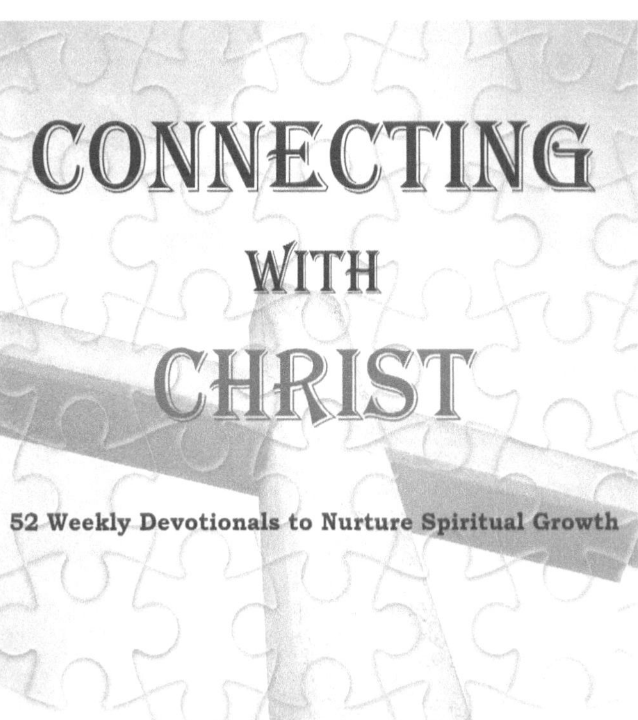

Edited By **Yolonda Tonette Sanders**

DiAnn Mills ◆ Cindy Thomson ◆ Leslie J. Sherrod
MaRita Teague ◆ Obieray Rogers
Sandra Merville Hart ◆ and others

A Yo Productions Publication

Excerpt from *Connecting with Christ* edited by
Yolonda Tonette Sanders

Introduction

If you conduct an internet search for devotionals, I'm sure that you won't find a shortage of materials. The challenge when constructing this project was creating something different enough to draw others' attention without requiring an enormous amount of time. The goal is not for anyone to spend an exorbitant amount of time with this devotional. As wonderful as this project is, nothing should replace the written Word of God contained in the Holy Bible. My prayer is that this work leads you to *the* Word and enhances your understanding of Scripture.

Enclosed you will find 52 devotionals broken into 12 themes to correlate with the 12 months of the year. Although the devotionals are ordered, feel free to go through the themes in a manner that best suits your needs. There is only one devotional per week. Ideally, the hope is that you will read the devotional at the beginning of the week and meditate on the Scripture and overall message for the rest of the week. You are encouraged to read the entire passages of the Scriptures listed to see what the Lord may reveal to you outside of what is written in this book. There is a place for you to jot down your thoughts each week if you choose.

You will notice that this work contains no dates, only generic weekly references (e.g., week 1). This is so you can use the entire collection of devotionals for many years to come. You do not have to follow the order of the weeks or themes. Go through this book as the Lord best leads you. May you hear His voice loud and clear as you journey on this road called life.

Love and Blessings,

Yolonda Tonette Sanders

Excerpt from *Connecting with Christ* edited by
Yolonda Tonette Sanders

Week 13: Revival

Change

by Obieray Rogers

"Do not be afraid, for I am with you; I will bring your children from the east and gather you from the west. I will say to the north, 'Give them up!' and to the south, 'Do not hold them back.' Bring my sons from afar and my daughters from the ends of the earth—everyone who is called by my name, whom I created for my glory, whom I formed and made."—Isaiah 43:5–7

The Bible holds many words that provide comfort and encouragement to give us hope in difficult circumstances. A review of newspaper headlines, reading articles online, or watching the news on the television should convince everyone that our world is in trouble. Global warming is real. Earthquakes, tornadoes, typhoons, and tsunamis are occurring more rapidly. Politicians appear to be increasingly unscrupulous. The pandemic, famine, and disease have changed all of our lives, and people are frustrated, angry, and mean*er*! There are days when reading or hearing the news makes you wonder what is going on and when the craziness will end.

If you're like me, you may even go as far as to say, *"Lord, come back now!"* The Bible is clear that none of us know when Jesus Christ will return (Matthew 24:36). What we do know is that the Bible has provided instructions on how to change God's mind: "If my people, who are called by my name, will humble themselves and pray and seek my face and turn from their wicked ways, then I will hear from heaven, and I will forgive their sin and will heal their land" (2 Chronicles 7:14).

It is a sad yet true fact that everyone won't follow the

instructions in the above Scripture because everyone doesn't believe in God. However, hope is not lost. To follow the directives of 2 Chronicles 7:14, one must first become a believer, and one of the ways to win souls is to pray. Isaiah 43:5–6 assures us that God will bring our children home when we ask. We all have parents, which makes us all children, and God has promised to bring the children back from the north, south, east, and west. Whether newly born or closing in on their 99th birthday, everyone who will accept the invitation is included in the promise. It doesn't matter what they've done, how they've lived, or whom they've hurt. God will bring them home! And, when that happens, the world will begin to heal. It may not happen overnight or in our lifetime, but as King David shared in Psalm 27:13, *"I remain confident of this: I will see the goodness of the* L ORD *in the land of the living."*

If we can hold onto the promise of Psalm 27:13, take 2 Chronicles 7:14 seriously, and believe Isaiah 43:5–6, the change *will* happen. The good news is that we can all participate in helping the change occur. God will always do His part to bring healing and restoration. He's waiting on us to do ours.

Lord, the world is in trouble, and we need a revival that can only come from You. Help us not to be selfish enough to pray only for the people we know and like. Help us to extend our prayers around the world to bring peace and order. We know You hear and see everything, so we believe it can and will be done. In Jesus's name, I ask these things. Amen.

Reflections

____

____

____

____